This book should be returned to any branch of the
Lancashire County Library on or before the date shown

2 8 JUL 2017

1 5 SEP 2017
2 5 FEB 2019
2 1 MAY 2021

First published in paperback in Great Britain 2017
by Egmont UK Limited
The Yellow Building, 1 Nicholas Road, London W11 4AN

Text copyright © 2017 Sam Watkins
Illustrations copyright © 2017 Vicky Barker
The moral rights of the author and illustrator have been asserted

ISBN 978 1 4052 8423 3

www.egmont.co.uk

65066/1

A CIP catalogue record for this title is available from the British Library

Printed and bound in Great Britain by the CPI Group

MIX
Paper
FSC FSC® C018306

CONTENTS

PHEE-WEEEEE, lovely humans! That's dolphin for 'hello' – just in case you forgot. I know you probably didn't forget, because human brains are nearly as big as dolphin brains. We dolphins have super-big brains, which is why I'm really good at writing and stuff. Dad said today I have **verbal diarrhoea**. I asked what that meant and he said it means I talk a lot and use a lot of words. Yay! So I've decided to try and use at least one new word every day from now on!

Gobbledegook

Skulduggery

Dugong

Gazump

I wrote so many words in my last diary that I filled it right up, so Mum bought me this new one. It is very shiny and lovely – and I already have some **mega-exciting** news to start it off . . .

WEEK 1:
Attack of the Zombie Crab

MONKFISHDAY

Tomorrow my new pen pal, Coral Crab, is coming to stay with me for three weeks! She lives in a place called Rockpool. Our head teacher, Mr Snapper, told us that because summer has been so hot, all the water in Rockpool School has dried up! So the pupils will come to our school until they get their water back. It's too far for them to go home every day, so everyone in my class has someone staying with them. It will be THE MOST FUN!! We've been writing sea-mails to get to know them.

Our teacher, Miss Carp, asked us to suggest ways we could make our visitors welcome. I was **bubbling** with ideas.

'A parade,' I said, 'with music and a synchronised swimming display ... and I could do a welcome speech ...'

Miss Carp said that sounded nice but really she meant little things like being kind to them, and asking what food they liked, what games they liked to play and stuff like that.

'I asked Melvin those things in my sea-mail,' my friend Ozzie Octopus said. 'Melvin's a mudskipper. He likes mud. So I've made a mud corner in the shipwreck, to help him feel at home.'

'Very thoughtful, Ozzie,' Miss Carp said. Myrtle Turtle put her fin up.

'My pen pal, Gloria Goby, likes painting and eating plankton,' she said. 'So Mum's bought plankton pasties and paints.'

'Excellent.' Miss Carp beamed. 'How about you, Darcy? What does your pen pal like?'

'Um . . .' I said. Luckily right then the bell rang. 'Oh – I just remembered – I have to go to the library.'

I shot out of the classroom. **Flippering fishsticks**, I wished I'd thought to ask Coral all those things! I was so busy telling her about me that I didn't think to ask about *her*!

In the library Miss Angler, the librarian, was sitting at her desk polishing her teeth. Miss Angler's teeth are razor-sharp and she is very strict, so I'm always very polite to her.

'Excuse me, Miss, and sorry to bother you
but do you have any books about crabs?' I
said, nervously.

Miss Angler glared at me, then swam off between the shelves, her little light dangling in front of her. A few minutes later she came back with a book. There was a scary-looking crab on the cover.

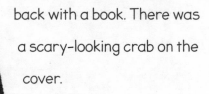

'*Attack of the Zombie Crabs*,' I read, 'by James Halibut.'

'A marvellous author,' said Miss Angler, smiling wickedly. 'I have all his books.'

Hmm. I wasn't sure if it was exactly what I needed – but I took it because it said 'A FIN-TINGLING READ' on the back.

I read the first chapter in bed and am now too scared to come out from under my bedcovers. Can crabs really come back to life as zombies? I really hope Coral doesn't do that sort of thing.

Word of the day: FIN-TINGLING
This means scary and exciting. I have to say that *Attack of the Zombie Crabs* is loads more scary than it is exciting.

TUNASDAY

Lots happened today! My pen pal, Coral Crab, is here. She's asleep now, in my bed. I'm sleeping with Remy, my pet remora, in his cave – such fun! Coral isn't quite what I expected – but I'll start at the beginning . . .

The Rockpool pupils arrived at the end of school. Just before the bell a sea urchin from the year below bounced into the classroom squeaking, 'They're here! They're here!'

'Wait quietly, everyone!' said Miss Carp, but no one did. We all rushed outside. The pen pals were in the playground, jostling about

nervously.

Ozzie waved a tentacle.

'Melvin!' he called.

A mud-brown fish with googly eyes swam

out of the crowd towards him. I saw a brightly

coloured fish dart across to Myrtle.

13

'Gloria! Wow, your colours are so pretty,' Myrtle said. Everyone started rushing about, finding their pen pals. But I couldn't see Coral, and the crowd of pen pals was getting smaller. Maybe she hadn't come after all?

'Darcy . . .'

I turned to see Miss Carp holding a large suitcase. Next to her was a small, red-brown crab with a scowl on her face as if she'd just trodden in sea-slug slime.

'This is Coral, Darcy,' Miss Carp said.

'Phee-weeeee!' I went to give her a hug, but she clicked her pincers at me. I stopped, looking nervously at the pincers.

'She was hiding under a rock,' Miss Carp whispered. 'Be patient, Darcy. I think she's shy.' She handed me the suitcase. 'Can you carry this for her? It's rather heavy.'

I took the suitcase, feeling sorry for the little crab. 'Come on, Coral. Let's go home.'

We set off, Coral scuttling sideways along the seabed. I soon stopped feeling sorry for her. She moaned and groaned the whole way!

'It's miiiiles to your house . . . my claws ache . . . are we nearly there yet?'

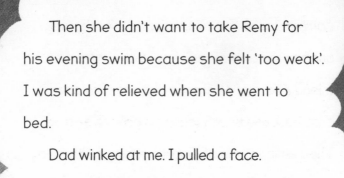

Then she didn't want to take Remy for
his evening swim because she felt 'too weak'.
I was kind of relieved when she went to
bed.

Dad winked at me. I pulled a face.

'Don't be crabby, Darcy,' he said, smirking.

Mum gave him a **Look**. 'Coral's probably
tired from her journey, sweetiefins. You wait –
she'll be a different crab in the morning.'

I really hope so – unless 'different' means

'zombie'! I read some

more *Attack of the*

Zombie Crabs this evening, and there's this one bit where the hero, Steve, thinks his best friend Zoe might have turned into a zombie crab because she moans and groans so much. This reminded me of Coral moaning on the way home and now I can't help wondering . . .

Word of the Day: CRABBY
I looked up 'crabby' in the dictionary. I thought it just meant 'like a crab' but it actually means 'bad-tempered'. ☺

WHALESDAY

Mum was wrong. Coral was **exactly** the same as yesterday. Plus she clicked her pincers in her sleep, which kept waking me up.

Coral grumbled all the way to school. When we finally got into class, Miss Carp gave us ten minutes to talk to our pen pals and find out some things they liked to do. I looked around to see how everyone else was getting on. Ozzie was showing Melvin a trick with his tentacles, and Gloria was giving Myrtle fashion tips.

Coral sat next to me with her pincers crossed, looking grumpy. Maybe we could play a game, I thought. What games might a crab like?

'Do you like Snap?' I asked.

She shrugged. 'Not really.'

'How about I Spy?'

She shook her head.

'Okay – what do you like to play?'

She flashed me a cheeky look.

'Clam Up.'

Finally – something Coral liked! 'Ooh, what's that?' I said.

'Both players shut their mouths for as long as they can. First person to talk loses.'

'Sounds fun!' I said, checking the clock. 'Ready, steady, GO!'

I shut my mouth. This was too easy! After a while I started feeling fidgety. My brain squirmed. My lips twitched. Words bubbled up in my mouth. I looked at the clock.

'One minute?!' I squeaked. 'I think the clock's stopped!'

Coral clicked her pincers in delight. 'I win.'

'That didn't count,' I said.

Coral just shrugged.

I felt more words bubble up in my mouth. Luckily before they could pop out Miss Carp clapped her fins.

'Lovely to see you all getting on so well,' she called and started handing out dictionaries.

'Persevere, Darcy,' she whispered to me as she swam past, putting a dictionary on my desk. I didn't know what that meant so I decided to look it up.

Then I remembered that Miss Carp

always says I have a **Positive Mental Attitude**.

I am the Positively Mental Darcy Dolphin!

I WILL MAKE CORAL LIKE ME.

EVERYTHING WILL BE OKAY!

Word of the Day: PERSEVERE

The dictionary says that this means trying hard to do something even if you find it really difficult. Like being nice to someone who may or may not be a zombie crab.

TURTLESDAY

I **persevered** so hard at being nice to Coral yesterday evening that I nearly exploded. Then I read two chapters of *Zombie Crabs* before bed. And you know what – Steve was right about Zoe – she IS a zombie crab! Steve is now trying to make his house zombie-proof, as he's scared Zoe will eat his brains! Apparently that is what zombies do. I peeked out of the toy cave at Coral and she looked fast asleep, but I put Remy on guard at the cave door, just in case.

24

In the middle of the night I was woken up by a fin-tingling noise.

Click-click, mooooooan, click-click, mooooooan . . .

click-click, mooooan, click-click...

It was Coral, clicking and moaning in her sleep again! Remy shot to my side and latched on, whimpering.

Maybe remoras don't make such great guard-fish.

I got up early and told Mum about Coral's moaning and clicking.

'She was probably having a nightmare, dear,' Mum said, trying to spoon prawnflakes into Diddy's mouth.

I gulped. Should I tell Mum my fears? I decided I had to.

'Mum . . . I think Coral might be a zombie crab,' I said. 'She's been acting really –'

'DIDDY! Don't throw your food!' Mum exclaimed suddenly as prawnflakes went flying. 'Sorry, Darcy darling, what was

that about Coral?'

I tried again. 'I think – in fact, I'm sure –
she's a zombie crab. She's going to try to eat
my brains. That's what zombies do. And I've got
an especially big brain.'

Mum laughed. 'Don't be silly, Darcy. Now
go and get Coral up or you'll both be late for
school – Diddy! Don't put prawnflakes in your
blowhole!'

Honestly, Mum doesn't understand how serious the situation is – just like Steve's mum in *Zombie Crabs!*

In class, Miss Carp had an announcement. 'Now, I thought it would be an idea if we put on a little talent show at the end of the visit. I want you to work with your pen pals on a five-minute act for the show. Working together – that's the important thing!'

I turned to Coral, who was making a pebble tower on her desk from pebbles she'd picked up on the way to school.

'Any ideas?' I asked.

Coral shrugged. 'I dunno.'

Persevere, Darcy, I said to myself.

'I know – we could do a dance?'

'I don't like dancing,' Coral said, reaching up to put another pebble on the tower. Something snapped inside me.

'Why are you so crabby?!' I shouted.
I pushed the tower and all the pebbles came tumbling down.

I felt bad as soon as I'd done it. 'I'm sorry . . . I didn't mean to do that. I just really want to be friends!'

I started trying to rebuild the tower, but Miss Carp had seen what happened and put me on Whale Cleaning Duty as a punishment. This means having to de-barnacle Walter the School Whale. Walter is lovely, but getting the cheeky barnacles off him is the worst job, and they call you rude names like 'stinking scurvy-ridden slimehead'.

Word(s) of the Day: Stinking scurvy-ridden slimehead

A slimehead is a type of fish. I'm not exactly sure what 'scurvy-ridden' means, but it must be rude because the barnacles laughed themselves silly.

FLOUNDERSDAY

O M G. Listen to this – I was just going into
the kitchen this morning when I heard Mum in
there talking to Coral.

'Would you like a brain, Coral?' she said.

My brain nearly exploded! Had Mum gone
mad? Where did she get a **brain** from?
Whose brain was it? And why was she offering
it to Coral for breakfast?!!!

I shot back into my room and flicked
through *Zombie Crabs* till I found the bit where
Zoe gets zombified. She is pinched by another

zombie crab, and thinks it isn't serious but it actually turns her into a zombie! I read the paragraph three times and decided there was a good chance that Coral had turned Mum into a zombie. I decided to keep a **close eye** on Mum from now on.

When I got back to the kitchen Coral had finished her breakfast, so I couldn't see if she had eaten brains or not, and I didn't dare ask.

I looked at Mum carefully, but she always looks a bit dead in the morning so it was hard to tell if she was a zombie or not. At lunchtime I managed to escape from Coral and found Ozzie and Myrtle. I told them my fears. Myrtle laughed.

'Zombie crabs aren't real, Darcy.'

Ozzie looked thoughtful. 'Actually I think I've heard of zombie crabs.'

'That proves it!' I cried. 'She's definitely a z–'

'Shhhh . . .' Ozzie put up a warning tentacle. I looked round to see Coral sidling up sideways behind me. Aargh. I really hope she didn't hear me. She didn't say anything, but I felt bad all afternoon.

I read chapter seven of *Zombie Crabs* before bed. Steve's the ONLY crab left who hasn't been zombified! In the book the zombie crabs are more active at night, just like Coral with her clicking and moaning. And she has now started sleep-crawling around the bedroom.

Flippering fishsticks – I could be in terrible danger!

Just in case Coral decides to turn me into a zombie tonight, here is a note for my loved ones:

Dear Loved Ones,

By the time you read this Coral will probably have turned me into a zombie. I did try to warn you she was a zombie crab but you wouldn't listen. I still love you all, though. Please don't feel guilty.

Best fishes,

Darcy xxx

Word of the Day: FLIPPERGASTED

This is the way you feel when you find out something shocking like your pen pal is actually a zombie crab who is trying to eat your brain. 😮

SALMONSDAY

Well, I'm happy to say that I'm still not a zombie, although Coral clicked and groaned all night and got up in a worse mood than EVER.

She grumped at everyone and upset Diddy. After an hour of this, Mum asked Coral if she wanted to go shopping. Coral shrugged, which Mum decided meant 'yes'.

'Coming, Darcy?' Mum asked. I was about to say 'yes' too (I love shopping!) but then I had an idea.

'Um, no, I think I'll stay in and do my homework,' I said. Mum gave me a very suspicious look, but Coral was already out of the door.

As soon as they'd both gone I raced into my room, Remy on my tail.

'Remy, I need proof that Coral is a zombie,' I said to him. He wagged his tail. 'Come on, help me find clues . . .'

I searched around the room, but couldn't

find anything zombie-like. Going through someone else's things felt a bit wrong though, and I was about to stop when Remy swam out from under the bed. He had something in his mouth.

'What's that?' I asked, taking it from him. It was lumpy and slightly pinky-grey, and looked like . . .

'A BRAIN!' I squeaked, dropping it immediately. Bleurgh!

It definitely looked like pictures of brains
I've seen in books.

I peered under the bed. There was a pile of
pebbles and rocks under there. Why did Coral
have loads of pebbles, I wondered? I couldn't
see any more brains.

But one brain was all the proof I needed.
I wrapped it in seaweed and swam over to
Myrtle's. She pulled a face when I showed her.

'Ew – that's gross! Maybe Coral is a
zombie crab, after all. But what can we do?'

'We should ask her straight out,' I said.
'She'll have to admit it, when she knows we've
found the brain.' I thought for a moment.
'I can't do it alone, though – just in case, you
know . . .'

'I've got an idea,' Myrtle said. 'You, Ozzie

39

and I could take a picnic to Ripple Rock with our pen pals. We can ask her there.'

'Bring sea squirts,' I said. 'If there's going to be a zombie crab **showdown** we'll need to defend ourselves.'

Word of the Day: SHOWDOWN

When you confront someone about something and then there's a lot of arguing and yelling but everything is okay afterwards. There is an awesomely shouty showdown in chapter eight of *Zombie Crabs*.

SPONGEDAY

I survived! Coral slept like a rock
for a change. Mum said she thought
Coral wasn't eating enough, so she
was happy for me to take her on a
picnic. I helped her make a stack of
sandwiches. I think I got a bit carried
away. I must have made about a
hundred.

Mum looked at them. 'Darcy, I
said to make CLAM sandwiches, not
Jiggling Jelly sandwiches!'

41

'Oh please, Mum . . . everyone loves Jiggling Jellies!'

The doorbell rang. It was Ozzie and Myrtle and their pen pals.

Mum sighed. 'Oh well, you'll have to take those ones I suppose.' She put them in a bag and gave them to me. 'Be NICE to Coral, Darcy.'

'Yes Mum,' I said. I thought I better not mention the zombie crab showdown.

When we arrived at Ripple Rock, I started unpacking the picnic. Coral said she wasn't hungry.

'They're Jiggling Jelly sandwiches,' I said. 'Everyone likes Jiggling Jellies.'

Coral sighed. 'I don't.'

I took a deep breath and glanced at Ozzie

and Myrtle. This was my chance. 'What do you like, Coral? Maybe ... **BRAINS**?'

I whipped the brain out. Coral's eyes nearly pinged out of her shell.

'What are you doing with Bertie?' she exclaimed.

'Don't deny it!' I cried. 'You're a zombie! You eat brains! I found this one under the bed – you were saving it for a snack, weren't you?!'

Coral snatched the brain off me.

'There, there, Bertie,' she said. 'I'll protect you from the crazy dolphin.'

'Help!' I hissed to Myrtle, but Ozzie stopped her. He swam over to Coral and peered at the brain.

'Darcy – that's not a brain,' he said. 'It's brain coral.'

I stared. 'Brain coral?'

'Yes,' Coral said. 'Bertie is a piece of dead brain coral. He's part of my rock and pebble collection.'

'You collect rocks?' I said, confused. 'Why didn't you tell me?'

'I did,' she said. 'But I don't think you were listening. You had your head buried in that zombie book.' She went on. 'Your mum found Bertie the other day. She knew I liked collecting stuff, so she gave him to me. He's the best thing in my collection.'

Waaaarrrggh! How stupid did I feel?! And I'd thought Mum was asking Coral if she

wanted a brain for **breakfast**. I looked at

Coral, who was patting Bertie gently with a

claw. I suddenly wondered if she was feeling

homesick for Rockpool. Maybe that was why

she was being grouchy. And I'd accused her

of being a zombie!

'I'm – I'm really

sorry I called you a

zombie crab,'

I said. 'It was stupid, and mean. Can we be . . .
friends?'

Coral looked at me warily.

'So . . . you don't think I'm crabby?' she
asked.

I thought. This was tricky. 'Well – a bit
maybe, but only as much as Mum when I don't
do my homework . . .'

Coral giggled suddenly. 'Bet my mum's
worse than yours,' she said. 'She's the Queen
of Crabbiness!'

We both laughed. Yay! At last we were
friends!

The rest of the picnic was fun. Coral tried
a Jiggling Jelly sandwich and liked it, and then
we all helped her collect some more rocks.
When we got home, she told me about every

47

single pebble in her collection in great detail. It

took two hours. I said I thought they were all

CRABULOUS.

Word of the Day: CRABULOUS

This is a word I invented. It means fabulous in a crabby sort of way. Coral said it was a good word.

    P.S. I have decided to take *Attack of the Zombie Crabs* back to the library. I think it's a bit silly, really. I mean, zombie crabs? Ha!

WEEK 2:
Pebble Pals

MONKFISHDAY

Hoo-RAY, a brand new day! I'm so happy Coral and I made friends yesterday. This morning when I went into the kitchen she actually said, 'Good morning, Darcy.' I was so **flippergasted** I almost forgot to answer, till Dad poked me.

'Oh yes, good moaning – morning – I mean,' I said, getting my prawnflakes.

Coral had a bowl already. Next to it sat her lump of brain coral. She held out a spoonful of prawnflakes.

'Eat up your breakfast, Bertie.'

Bertie sat in stony silence.

I giggled. 'I don't think rocks like prawnflakes.'

'He's coral, actually,' Coral said. 'Don't hurt his feelings.'

'Dead coral,' I said. 'So really he's a rock. And rocks don't have feelings.'

Coral glared. 'How do you know how rocks feel?'

'Because –' I said, then saw Mum wagging her fin at me. I remembered that Coral might be feeling homesick. 'You're right. I don't know how rocks feel. Oh Remy, stop that!'

Remy had darted over and snaffled all the prawnflakes off Coral's spoon. Coral clicked her pincers at him and he shot under the table, cheeks bulging.

'Don't scare Remy,' I said. 'He's very
sensitive.'

'He ate Bertie's breakfast!'

'Bertie didn't want his breakfast!' I said,
crossly.

'Silly old wock,' said Diddy, whacking Bertie
with his spoon. Coral grabbed Bertie, looking
like she was about to explode. Mum told us all to
stop it THIS INSTANT or she would blah blah
blah etc.

Oh dear. Coral wouldn't speak to me all the way to school. I tried to make friends again by asking what she wanted to do in the talent show, but she just grunted 'Dunno' and that was that ☹.

The day hadn't got off to a good start. But it got better. After register, Miss Carp told us that tomorrow was **Show and Tell** day.

'Ooooh-WHEEEEEEE!' I squealed. Show and Tell days are my favourite days EVER!!!!! You can bring a special object to school and talk about it. I asked Coral what she was going to bring in.

'Bertie, of course,' she said, smiling at him. 'And maybe some of my other pebbles.'

She's dotty about that bit of rock! This evening she put him to bed early for 'his big day tomorrow'. I thought about what to take till my brain ached, but I just couldn't think of anything.

Word of the Day: ECCENTRIC

I heard Mum say to Dad that Coral was just a little 'eccentric' so I looked it up and it means someone who does sort of odd things. Like talk to bits of rock.

TUNASDAY

Show and Tell day! I got up early to find something to take into school but Remy kept distracting me by chasing his tail. I laughed at him whizzing round in circles.

'Funny thing – you'll never catch it!' Then I had an idea. 'Remy! I can take YOU in! You're not exactly an object, but you're special.'

Coral was in the bathroom, brushing Bertie's 'teeth'.

'Are you excited about coming to school?' she asked him. He didn't look that excited to me.

When we got to school everyone was showing each other their special things. I tied Remy to my desk and tried to catch Miss Carp's eye. I really wanted to go first, so I sat as still as Bertie. Finally she looked up.

'Stop fidgeting, Darcy,' she said.

I stopped. 'Miss, please may I –'

'Not now, Darcy. It's Show and Tell time! First up is . . .'

ME! ME! ME! I shouted (in my head of course).

'. . . Ozzie Octopus.'

Hmmmf. I slumped back down. Ozzie showed a gold medallion that he found in the shipwreck where he lives. He said it was pirate gold! Next up was Melvin, Ozzie's pen pal. He showed a fossilised mudskipper. He said it was

one of his ancestors called Tony. I felt sure it
would be me next. . .

'Angie Angelfish,' Miss Carp called.

Sigh. Angie showed her seahorse riding
trophy collection. Then Clara Cod, then
Raymond Ray, then Myrtle and Gloria . . . in
fact **EVERYONE** went before me and Coral.
Finally Miss Carp looked at us.

'Next up is . . .'

I grabbed Remy.

'Coral Crab,' Miss Carp said.

Fishsticks! I wasn't going to get a go at this rate. Coral went to the front of the class with her pebbles. She held each one up and talked about it. Then she held up Bertie.

'Bertie is my favourite. He is a piece of dead brain coral. Bertie likes to eat prawnflakes. He doesn't like parrotfish because they eat coral –'

I accidentally yawned. Coral glared at me, and held Bertie up to her ear.

'What's that, Bertie? You're not that keen on dolphins either?'

I snorted (not accidentally).

'Darcy, it's rude to snort,' Miss Carp said.

Angie Angelfish put her fin up. 'Does he like angelfish?'

Coral held Bertie to her ear. 'Yes, he likes angelfish.'

Angie smirked at me.

Suddenly every fin in class shot up! Everyone wanted to see if Bertie liked them.

By the time it was my turn to Show and Tell, there was only five minutes till lunch, so I hardly got to talk about Remy at all. Luckily Remy didn't mind. He had caught his tail and was trying to eat it.

Word of the Day: DEFLATED

This is like when all the air goes out of a pufferfish. And that is how I feel now. Like a deflated pufferfish.

WHALESDAY

When we got into school this morning, I saw Coral getting Bertie out of her bag. I was about to ask why she'd brought him in again, when I heard a voice.

'Coral...?'

Angie Angelfish and her pen pal, Lenny Blenny, were hovering about in front of Coral's desk.

'We wanted some dead coral but couldn't find any,' Angie said. 'But we found some nice pebbles instead. This is Pinkie.'

She placed a large pink pebble in front of
Bertie. Lenny put a pebble next to Pinkie.
'And this is Pebsy.'

'They want to be friends with Bertie,' said
Angie.

Coral looked pleased. She picked Bertie up
and put him to her ear. 'Bertie says he'd like
that!'

'Oh come on –' I began, but before I could
finish our desk was **swamped** with pupils.
Everyone was waving some sort of rock or
pebble at Coral.

'Mine's The Rock,' said Arnold
Anchovy.

'Mr Mussel,' said Steven
Stingray, holding up a big rock
covered in black mussels.

'Wow, he's really mussely,' Angie said admiringly. I rolled my eyes.

Coral looked at all the pebbles, rocks and bits of coral sitting on her desk.

'Bertie has so many new pals now!' she said happily.

'I know – we'll call them Pebble Pals,' said Angie.

Just then Miss Carp swam in. 'To your desks, everyone!' Everyone quickly swam back to their seats. 'Before we begin, a reminder about the Talent Show. I hope you are all getting lots of practice in . . .'

Flippering fishsticks – I'd forgotten all about that! We still hadn't even decided what to do. At lunchtime I tried to get Coral to talk about it, but she

said she was going to play
with Angie and Lenny.

Feeling a bit upset, I went to
find Myrtle and Ozzie. They'd been at finball
practice all morning so I hadn't seen
them, but I was sure they wouldn't
have …

'Hey, Darcy,' Myrtle said as I swam
up. 'Meet Barnacle Bill.'

She held out a black pebble with a few
barnacles on it. One of the barnacles stuck its
tongue out at me.

Ozzie held out a lump of rock. 'Indiana
Stones.'

I couldn't speak. Everyone except me must have a Pebble Pal now!

'Where's yours, Darcy?' said Myrtle, patting Barnacle Bill.

I muttered something about not being that bothered about Pebble Pals, and then swam off and left them to their silly rocks.

I am NOT getting a Pebble Pal.

No way.

End. Of. Story.

Word of the Day: CODSWALLOP
This has nothing to do with walloping cod. It means a load of rubbish or nonsense. Like everyone getting rocks and calling them things like 'Pinkie' and 'Pebsy'.

TURTLESDAY

Guess what? I now have a Pebble Pal!

I know I said I wouldn't get one. But at lunchtime today Myrtle and Ozzie and their pen pals were playing a game with their Pebble Pals. Coral and Angie Angelfish were playing too. I asked if I could join in. Coral looked at Angie.

'Only people with Pebble Pals can play,' Angie said bossily.

'Why don't you get one, Darcy?' Ozzie whispered. 'Then you can play.'

I said I would watch. Pebble Pals – so silly!
But it did look kind of fun. I looked around. Most
of the big pebbles had been taken, but I found
a tiny bit of grey rock in a corner. It looked sort
of lonely and left out. A bit like me.

I picked it up and swam back to the game.

'This is, um . . . Chip.' I said, holding out my
bit of rock.

Coral squinted at it. 'He's a bit . . . small, isn't he?' she said.

'More gravel than pebble,' Angie added, sniggering.

Some not very polite words bubbled up in my mouth. Ozzie came to my rescue.

'It doesn't matter how big he is! Come on Darcy, you and Chip can play.'

Angie glared at him. 'Coral and I invented Pebble Pals, so we should set the rules,' she said. 'Right, Coral? Pebble Pals should be a certain size?'

Coral looked awkwardly at me. 'Well, I suppose . . .'

'There!' Angie said triumphantly. 'Sorry, Darcy.'

I was about to blow my blowhole, but

Myrtle grabbed me.

'Okay Angie,' Myrtle said. 'We'll play with Darcy, and you and Coral can play your own game with your rules.'

'Fine!' Angie went lobster red. 'But our Pebble Pals are NOT friends with yours!'

She stormed off. Coral hesitated. For a minute I thought she was going to stay with us. But then Angie had to come back for her pebble (which hadn't stormed off, because pebbles can't storm off).

'Come ON, Coral!' Angie hissed. Coral turned and followed Angie.

That was the start of the **Great Pebble War**. All of the rest of lunchtime a battle raged between our Pebble Pals and Coral and Angie's Pebble Pals. Soon almost everyone

in school had taken sides. I really don't like wars and fighting and stuff. And I felt really upset that Coral had sided with Angie.

So when we got home I told Coral I thought the **Pebble War** was silly and we should stop it.

'And – why did you go off with Angie?' I said. 'I thought we were friends?'

Coral pulled a face. 'I don't know ... you were mean about Bertie. And Angie was nice to him.'

'I wasn't mean –' I suddenly remembered telling her rocks didn't have feelings. 'Okay – sorry. I guess I was a bit mean. But you and Angie were mean not to let Chip play the game just because he's little.'

Coral looked like she was going to say something, but stopped. To my surprise, at dinner time she made Bertie give Chip a bit of fish finger. If Bertie and Chip are friends, does that mean me and Coral are friends again too, I wonder?

Word of the Day: TRUCE

A truce is when you are having an argument
with someone but then both of you decide
to stop arguing and maybe offer each other
presents like bits of fish finger to show you are
friends again. ☺

FLOUNDERSDAY

Coral and I actually talked to each other on the way to school! As we arrived, Coral was saying that Bertie could help Chip with his spelling.

'And Chip can help Bertie with his numbers,' I said. 'Wait – what's that noise?'

A **rock-splitting** din was coming from the classroom. I opened the door and my eyes nearly swam out of my head.

What a **kerfuffle!** Everyone was screeching at each other and Pebble Pals were flying about everywhere.

Coral and I looked at each other.

'Miss Carp will be here any minute,' I said. 'We've got to make them stop!'

'I've got an idea.' Coral climbed on a desk, and held Bertie up.

'Coo-ee! Bertie wants you all to make friends!' she called.

No one heard her – and right at that moment, I saw a Pebble Pal sailing towards Coral. With a flick of my tail, I knocked it away just in time! But I also knocked Bertie out of Coral's claw. He spun off towards the door . . .

The door opened.

'WHAT IS GOING ON?'

It was Mr Snapper, the head teacher.

Everyone froze . . . except Bertie.

He kept sailing straight
towards
Mr Snapper's head
. . . closer . . . and
closer . . .

SNAP!

Mr Snapper caught
Bertie neatly between
his teeth.

He took Bertie out of his mouth.

'So this is one of these . . . Pebble Pals?' he
said in a **scary** voice. 'Whose is it?'

Silence. Coral put one trembly claw up.

'M-mine, sir. His name is Bertie. I didn't
mean to –'

'Wait!' I couldn't let Coral take the blame.
'It was my fault, sir,' I said. 'I knocked him out

of Coral's claw. I'm sorry.'

Mr Snapper nodded. 'I see. Well, Bertie is going to have to wait outside the school gate till the end of the day. Along with all the other Pebble Pals. Darcy and Coral, you will stay behind after school to help Miss Carp tidy up.'

Coral moped about Bertie all day. She even wrote him a letter and posted it through the gate at lunchtime.

DEAR BERTIE,
I HOPE YOU ARE NOT TOO LONELY WITHOUT ME. I WILL SEE YOU SOON.
LUV,
CORAL X

After helping Miss Carp tidy up, Coral and I rushed outside to find Bertie. As we got near the gate, Coral gave a cry.

My Pebble Pal, Chip, was sitting there on his own. All the other Pebble Pals had gone. And Bertie was nowhere to be seen!

Word of the Day: ROCKNAPPED

Coral says Bertie has been **rocknapped**. This is when horrid people steal a rock and then ask for loads of money before they give it back. Maybe the letter asking for money will come tomorrow. I hope they don't ask for too much – I only have five squid in my squiddybank!

SALMONSDAY

Last night was difficult. Coral was soooo upset about Bertie being **rocknapped**. Dad tried to cheer her up.

'How many tickles does it take to make an octopus laugh?'

There was a gloomy silence. 'I don't know,' Coral said at last in a very quiet voice.

'Ten tickles! Get it? Tentacles! Ha ha ha!' Dad looked **REALLY** pleased with himself.

After that Coral went into the bedroom and wouldn't come out. I tried to get her to talk about what we could do for the Talent Show to take her mind off Bertie, but she said she had a shell-ache.

This morning we still had not had a letter from the rocknappers. Dad said probably Bertie hadn't been rocknapped and was just lost. Mum made tubeworms on toast (Coral's favourite) but Coral said she couldn't eat, knowing that Bertie was out there somewhere, alone and scared. Her face started wobbling.

'Don't cry,' I said anxiously. 'Look – you can have Chip if you like. You'd be better at looking after him than me anyway.'

Coral shook her head. 'Thank you,' she said sadly. 'But I just want Bertie back.'

I tried to think what might cheer her up. I was about to suggest rock collecting, but then thought maybe that wasn't a good idea what with Bertie going missing and everything. I realised I still didn't really know what else Coral liked doing.

'Shall we have a look round the shops?' I asked.

Coral heaved a big sigh. 'All right.'

Ripple Reef Shopping Centre was really busy. We wandered around, Coral trailing along behind me like a piece of sad seaweed. I was beginning to think we should go home, when I

spotted my favourite shop EVER.

'Ooh, let's go to Flotsam,' I said. 'They have

some really cool stuff.'

Flotsam sells stuff like lampshades and toilet-roll holders and hats. We swam over. A sign on the door read **CLOSED TILL SPONGEDAY**.

'Bother!' I said, looking in the window. And then I saw something I KNEW Coral would like. 'Oh look, Coral – some pretty pebbles!'

Coral peered into the window. Suddenly she made a strangled noise.

'What's the matter?' I said and Coral waved a claw at the pebbles. I looked again.

Sitting in the middle of the pebbles was a big pinky-white piece of coral. It looked sort of like ... a **BRAIN!**

'Bertie!' I exclaimed in delight. Then my heart sank.

There was a label on him. It said:

SOLD.

☹

Word of the Day: FLUMMOXED

Flummoxed is when you are so surprised by something you can hardly speak. This does not happen very often to me but it did today when I saw the 'SOLD' sign on Bertie.

SPONGEDAY

Coral was still miserable yesterday evening. She said it was great that we'd found Bertie, but how could we get him back? In bed, I came up with a **Good Idea**, which I announced at breakfast this morning.

'We'll buy Bertie back!'

Coral stared. 'I don't have any money. Anyway, he's been sold to someone else.'

I fetched my squiddybank. 'There's five squid in here – that's loads. We'll tell the shop owner he's yours and that you have to have him back.'

Breakfast took foreeeeeeever. Finally Mum let us go, and we raced to the shop. As we got there I saw Sam Swordfish, the shop owner, in the window. And – **horror of horrors** – he was taking Bertie off the pile of pebbles!

'Quick!' I said. We swam in. A little old ladyfish was waiting at the counter while Sam wrapped Bertie in a piece of seaweed.

'ROCKNAPPERS!' Coral cried.

Sam and the ladyfish turned, surprised.

'What she means is, we want . . . we need
– we HAVE to buy that piece of coral,' I said
quickly.

'Impossible. I have bought it already,' said
the ladyfish.

'But it belongs to my friend,' I said,
desperately. 'She had to leave it outside the
school gate, and when we went back later, it
had gone!'

Sam nodded. 'That's where I found it,'
he said. 'Dead brain coral is hard to find. Of
course, I never take living coral. I didn't know it
belonged to someone.'

The ladyfish sniffed. 'Well, I've paid five
squid for it now.'

Coral's face started to crumple. I pushed
my five squid towards the ladyfish.

'I'll pay you for it!'

'But I want it for my knick-knacks shelf!'

she exclaimed.

'WAAAHHHHHHHH!' Coral

burst into tears.

'She's very attached to Bertie,' I said.

The ladyfish looked puzzled. 'Who is
Bertie?'

'The coral,' I said. 'And he's missing her,
too. He's sad.'

'Sad?' said the ladyfish, astonished. 'Rocks
don't have feelings, my dear.'

I glared at her. '**How do you know
how rocks feel?**'

Coral was so surprised by me saying that,
she stopped crying. The ladyfish's eyebrows
shot up.

I took a deep breath. 'Sorry but it's really
important you give Bertie back because Coral
is homesick and she likes collecting rocks and
then Mum found Bertie which made her happy
but I was mean about him and then we had

a Pebble War but Bertie made friends with Chip but the next day everyone was yelling which made Mr Snapper cross and . . .'

'Stop!' The ladyfish mopped her brow. 'Well. I didn't quite follow all that, but I can see how much it means to you, my dears.'

She unwrapped Bertie and handed him to Coral. Coral was so delighted she could hardly speak. She just gazed at Bertie adoringly.

'You've got a very good friend here,' the ladyfish said to Coral. 'Friends are so important. Much more important than lumps of rock ...'

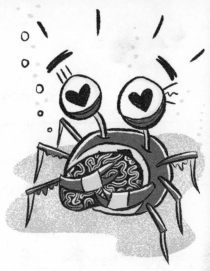

I had to drag Coral out of the shop at that point, before she said something not very polite.

But all's swell that ends swell! (That's a quote from William Sharkspeare, by the way.)

Word of the Day: REUNITED

When two people (or a person and a rock) have got lost from each other and then they find each other again. Hurrah!

WEEK 3:
A Little Bit of Magic!

MONKFISHDAY

EEEEEEEEK! This is the last week

that Coral will be here – which means we've

only got **ONE** week to get ready for the

Talent Show on Salmonsday. What with all the

Pebble Pals kerfuffle last week, we hadn't even

decided what to do.

'I wrote a song for Bertie last night, to

welcome him home,' Coral said this morning.

'It's a rock song. We could sing it for the Talent

Show.'

'Cool!' I said, surprised but pleased.

'Go on, then!'

Coral started singing, in a very high and

screechy voice.

Rocks are lurv-e-ly, rocks are GREAT!
Some are curv-e-ly, some are STRAIGHT!
Rocks are rocky, can't you see . . .
Rocks are good for you and ME!

Remy shot into his cave with his fins over his ears and a pained look on his face. I must have had the same look, because Coral stopped singing.

'What's wrong?' she said, crossing her claws and glaring at me.

'Nothing . . . only, it's not really a rock song, is it? It's a song ABOUT rocks.'

'You don't like it, do you?'

'No – I mean, YES! I like it. It's very . . .' I tried to think of something good about it. 'Short.'

Coral was in a huff with me all the way to school. Then, in assembly, Mr Snapper said he had an **important announcement**.

'Simon Trout will be judging the Ripple Reef Talent Show.'

SIMON TROUT?! An astonished murmur went round the hall. Next to me, Myrtle gasped, and Ozzie went pink and green.

I thought I was going to faint. Angie did faint.

Simon Trout is a really, really Big Fish. He is the judge on a TV talent show called Starfish in Their Eyes. He's also really, really hard to please if he's in a **Bad Mood**. But why was he coming to judge our little talent show?

It was like Mr Snapper read my mind because he said, 'Simon Trout used to go to this school. So I sea-mailed him to see if he'd come and judge the show, and to my surprise, he said yes!'

Starfish in Their Eyes was on TV this evening so I watched it with Coral, Mum and

Dad. The acts were all clam-azing, but Simon

Trout must have been in one of his famous

Bad Moods because he looked mega-

grumpy and gave everyone really low marks.

A jellyfish band called Well-Jel did an awesome

lightshow, and Simon Trout gave them three

out of ten. He said he'd seen sea squirts with more talent.

I gulped. What would he say to Coral's singing? Probably that it sounds like a seagull with a sore throat!

I turned to Coral. 'We can't do your rock song. It's too . . . um . . . short.'

Coral is now in the bedroom writing another verse. We are **doomed**.

Word of the Day: DOOMED

'Doomed' in this case means 'Simon Trout will eat us alive'.

TUNASDAY

This morning at school Miss Carp let everyone
go off to practise their acts. Coral wanted
me to hear her second verse, but I said we
should check out the competition first. In the
playground we found Ozzie's pen pal, Melvin.
He was swimming slowly round a treasure
chest, carrying a drum.

'Where's Ozzie?' I asked.

Melvin started to beat the drum slowly.

A tentacle appeared through a small hole in
the chest lid. The drum got faster and faster.

Another tentacle appeared . . . then another . . .
Finally Ozzie's whole body squeezed through.
Melvin dropped the drumsticks and collapsed
in an exhausted heap. A crowd of sardines
clapped and cheered loudly. It was pretty
impressive, I have to say.

Next we went into the school hall. Myrtle
and Gloria were parading up and down the
stage in gorgeous multi-coloured seaweed
costumes.

'We're doing a fashion show,' Myrtle said. 'Gloria designed everything.'

Angie Angelfish and her pen pal, Lenny Blenny, were doing an acrobatics routine. Everyone seemed to have found something really good to do.

Everyone except us. 😵😞

That evening Coral cornered me in the bedroom.

'Darcy, we have to practise,' she said.

I sighed. 'Okay.'

'You can sing the second verse,' Coral said, handing me the song sheet.

I started singing.

'ROCKS ARE HEEERE AND ROCKS ARE THEEERE . . . ROCKS ARE ALMOST

– what's the matter?'

Coral had her pincers over her ears. Remy was looking at me in terror. The bedroom door burst open and Mum's head poked in.

'Darcy! What was that awful screeching? Are you hurt?'

'I wasn't screeching, I was singing,' I

said, crossly. Mum said well could I screech
– sorry – sing a bit quieter please because
I was scaring Diddy. And the rest of the
neighbourhood.

When she'd gone, Coral looked at me
ruefully. 'I guess we can't do the song if we
can't practise it.'

'No,' I said, relieved. 'But what CAN we do?'

Word of the Day: INSPIRATION
Dad said we just needed some **INSPIRATION**.
I thought that must be some sort of medicine
but I looked it up and it means having a
Really Brilliant Idea.

WHALESDAY

After racking my brains all day and having no inspirations whatsoever, I called an **emergency brainstorm** meeting. Mum and Dad were watching TV.

'I know,' I said. 'I'll make a list of things I'm good at, and you make one too and we'll see if there's anything that comes up on both!'

My list went like this:

<u>Things I Am Good At</u>

1. Wave-jumping

2. Helping people

3. Talking

4. Making friends

5. Eating 67 Jiggling Jellies in one minute
   (that's probably the World Record!)

6. Echolocation*
   *This is a way of finding things by
   clicking and listening for the echo –
   dolphins are fintastic at this!

Coral's list went like this:

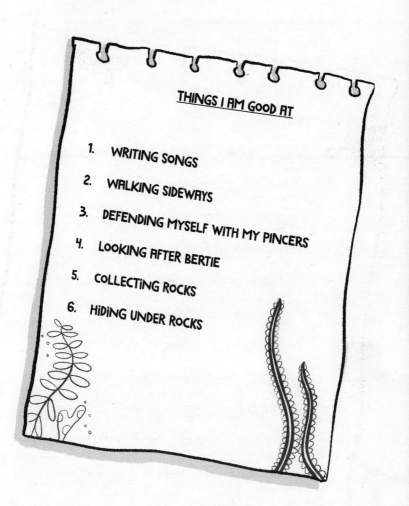

THINGS I AM GOOD AT

1. WRITING SONGS
2. WALKING SIDEWAYS
3. DEFENDING MYSELF WITH MY PINCERS
4. LOOKING AFTER BERTIE
5. COLLECTING ROCKS
6. HIDING UNDER ROCKS

'Hmm,' I said. 'You can't really hide under a rock for a talent show.'

Coral looked at my list. 'You can't just help people, either.'

'Why not?'

'Well . . .' She looked doubtful. 'It wouldn't be very interesting to watch.'

I sighed. 'I guess you're right.'

Dad looked over.

'Still no inspiration, girls? How about doing some stand-up comedy?'

'What's that?' I asked.

'Telling jokes on stage. Like . . . why did the lobster run away?'

'Don't know,' Coral and I said at the same time.

'Because it saw anemone. An enemy – get it?!'

We both groaned. Coral said she didn't think she would be much good at telling jokes.

'I know – juggling,' she said.

'Can you juggle?'

'No.'

'Well that's a silly idea then,' I said impatiently.

'Have you got a better one?' Coral snapped. Mum looked round.

'Are you girls still at it? I thought you had made friends! It will take nothing less than magic to stop you two arguing.'

DING! I had a whale-sized inspiration.

'We can do a **magic show**! No one else is doing that.'

Coral looked unsure. 'But we don't know any magic tricks!'

'There's bound to be a book on magic in the school library,' I said. 'We'll go tomorrow and ask Miss Angler.'

'I know a good magic trick,' Dad said. 'I can make you two girls disappear. What do you call a fish with no eyes?'

'Come on Coral,' I whispered, and we shot out of the room.

'Told you I could make you disappear!' Dad called after us.

Word of the Day: FSH

This is what you call a fish with no eyes,

apparently.

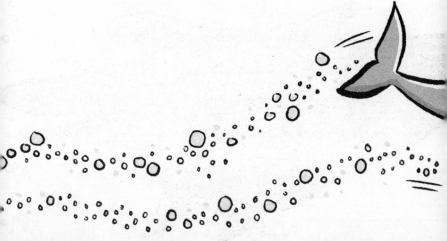

TURTLESDAY

Wee-hee! We have a super-fab idea for the Talent Show ☺. Now we just have to learn some magic tricks, get magic equipment and practise till we're really good. Three days is loads of time . . .

'Three days is not long to learn the Art of Magic, Darcy,' Miss Carp said when I asked her if Coral and I could go to the library at lunchtime for a magic book. 'Wouldn't you be better off doing something a bit simpler? Maybe a mime act?'

I asked whatever had happened to her
Positively Mental Attitude and she put me on
Whale Cleaning Duty for being cheeky, but
luckily she let me go to the library first.

Miss Angler gave me a book called *Magic
for Dummies*. I wasn't too happy about that
but she said it just meant the tricks were
easy. Coral agreed to come with me on Whale
Cleaning Duty and read the contents page
while I prized barnacles off Walter's tail.

'Eel-tying tricks . . . rabbitfish in a hat
tricks . . . cutting someone in half tricks –'

'That sounds good,' I called.

·MOULDY OLD MUDSUCKER!·

squeaked a barnacle as I pinged it off into the blue.

'You're not cutting me in half,' Coral called
back.

'Okay, okay!'

Coral continued reading. 'Disappearing acts . . .'

I felt a buzz of excitement. 'That would impress Simon Trout!'

Coral went on. 'Dazzle your audience by making a prawn vanish before their eyes . . .'

'A prawn?' My heart sank. 'I was thinking something more like . . .' I looked at Walter. 'A whale.'

'What?' Coral looked at me, astonished.

'What?' Walter echoed, swivelling one

huge, startled eye

towards me.

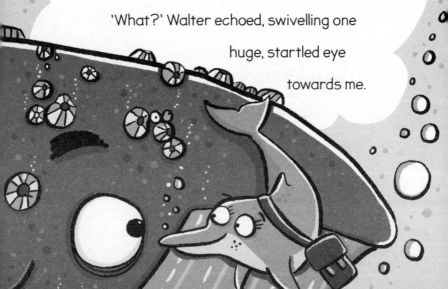

'How can we make a whale disappear?'
Coral demanded.

'Same way as a prawn, I guess! What do
you think, Walter?'

Walter said he would love to help, but some
sardines had already asked him to help them
with their performance of *Moby Dick*.

To be honest, disappearing a whale might
be quite tricky. What's smaller than a whale but
bigger than a prawn? I looked at Coral.

WHALE

PRAWN

'No,' Coral said. 'No, no and no.'

I had to promise to go rock collecting with her every day before she finally agreed to be disappeared.

Word of the Day: WOOFLE DUST
Special invisible magic stuff that magicians use to make things disappear. I'm not sure if I'll be able to get any of it so I'll just have to pretend.

FLOUNDERSDAY

Coral woke up super-grouchy.

'My shell aches,' she grumbled at breakfast. 'I don't want to go to school.'

'We're practising our act today,' I said. 'You won't have to do much. It's me that has the hard job!'

First we had to collect some equipment. Mum gave me an old seaweed curtain. She suggested we ask Aunt Ditzy for a magician's hat and a wand.

Aunt Ditzy has a whole cave full of hats

and stuff, and she found us an old wizard's hat. She didn't have a wand but said she'd see what she could do. We also collected some rocks and seaweed on the way to school.

Miss Carp said we could practise on the stage in the hall. It was empty, except for a group of sardines reading in a corner, who started pointing at us and whispering.

'What are you looking at?' Coral snapped. She was in an especially bad mood today – I thought it must be because of her shell-ache. The sardines quickly stuffed their heads back in their books.

I opened *Magic for Dummies*, turned to the vanishing trick page and read the instructions. It seemed easy enough.

'Right,' I said. 'We arrange the rocks behind you to look like they're just part of the backdrop. I hold the cloak up, then when you hear me say **'VANISHING CRAB'**, run behind the nearest rock and cover yourself with seaweed for extra disguise. You look a bit like a rock too – just make sure you keep extra still.'

We arranged the rocks at the back of the stage and I held the seaweed curtain up in front of Coral.

'Ladies and Jellyfish! I present – the One – the Only – the Incredible . . . **VANISHING CRAB!**'

'A-A-A-AARRRGHHH!'

I looked round. Coral had fallen off the back
of the stage.

'Oh, fishsticks . . .'

The sardines exploded into fits of giggles.
I swam over and pulled a groaning Coral up.

'Don't go so far back,' I said. 'Stand just
behind the curtain. Okay – let's try again.'

I held up the curtain.

'. . . **VANISHING CRAB!**'

I whipped the curtain away.

R-R-R-R-R-R-RIPPPPPPPPPPPP!

Coral's pincer caught in the curtain and it tore
right down the middle.

'Fishsticks!' I cried, again. 'You were too
far forward this time!'

'Hey! You've wrecked my home!' came a tiny, angry voice.

A very brightly-coloured mantis shrimp shot out of the ripped curtain and **thwacked** Coral hard on the nose. Mantis shrimps are small but deadly. One thwack can knock you out for a week.

'YOOOWW!' Coral howled.

I tried to grab the furious shrimp but it thwacked me too. The sardines rolled about laughing.

'WHAT'S THIS RACKET?!'

Miss Angler,

the scary librarian, burst in, gnashing her
long sharp teeth, and herded the terrified
sardines off. The mantis shrimp
disappeared in a flash of
rainbow colours.

I held up the two
pieces of curtain.

'Um . . . are you any good at
sewing?' I asked. Coral is now not
speaking to me again. ☹

Word of the Day: FISHSTICKS

I know I say 'fishsticks' a lot, so it's not really

a new word, but today was an especially

fishsticky day.

SALMONSDAY

The Big Day! We arrived at the theatre to find Aunt Ditzy waiting outside the stage door. She gave me a long, thin package.

'What is it . . . oh!' I gasped, as I opened it. A **magic wand!** I waved it, and a plankton on the end lit up!

'Wow, thanks, Aunt Ditzy,' I said. I had a wand! Now I was a PROPER magician!

We had to wait backstage for ages, but finally the show started. Angie and Lenny were on first. They were really nervous, and every time Lenny tried to balance Angie on his nose she fell off. Everyone waited anxiously to hear what Simon Trout would say. He scribbled on his clipboard, then held it up.

'Simon says . . . Eight out of Ten.'

'He must be in a **Good Mood!**' I put my wizard's hat on and grabbed the wand and curtain. 'Come on Coral, it's our turn.'

'I don't feel well,' Coral moaned.

'This is no time for stage fright . . .' Miss Carp bustled us on stage. Simon Trout waved at me to begin.

'LADIES AND JELLYFISH –'

'Oi! Keep the noise down!'

An angry little face peered over the brim of my hat. The mantis shrimp! I glared at it.

'What are you doing in my hat?'

'Trying to have a lie-in!' the shrimp
squeaked. 'Flippin' impossible, round here!'

'Come along please,' Simon Trout called.
'We haven't got all day!'

I gulped. 'LADIES AND JELLYFISH,
PREPARE TO BE –'

'– KARATE CHOPPED!' shrieked the shrimp. To my horror, it hurled itself straight towards Simon Trout, and – **THWACK!** – karate chopped him on the nose.

'**YOOOooowwwwWW!**' howled
Simon Trout. The shrimp thwacked him again.
And again. It took three lobsters to make it
stop thwacking and seven damselfish to settle
the red-faced judge back down. Simon Trout
was now in a Bad Mood.

'GET ON WITH IT!' he roared.

I got on with it. 'Meet the – um – famous
VANISHING CRAB . . .'

I held the curtain up in front of Coral and
waved my wand.

'CRAB-RA-CAD-ABRA!'

I whipped the curtain away,
to reveal . . .

Coral. Completely
un-vanished.

The audience giggled. Simon Trout shook his head and wrote something on his clipboard.

I stared at her. 'What are you doing?!'

She didn't speak. Or move. She looked strange – almost zombie-like . . .

'Coral?' I poked her gently with the wand.

There was a flash of light from

the plankton on the

end. And then, with

a shudder, Coral

collapsed into a pile

of bits of shell!

The giggling stopped.

I stared at my wand, then at

what was left of Coral.

'Er, is this part of the act?' Simon Trout

asked, looking round uncertainly.

I panicked. **I'VE KILLED HER!** I

cried. 'I poked her with my magic wand and

now she's –'

'Coo-eee!' called a voice from behind me.

I turned. A bright pink crab was skipping out

from behind the pile of rocks! I looked at the stranger blankly.

'Who are you? What's going on?' I spluttered. 'Have you crab-napped Coral?!'

The pink crab laughed. 'No silly – I AM Coral!'

I gasped. It did sound like Coral. But . . .

'What . . . I mean how . . . ?' I stared at the bits of shell on the stage, lost for words.

'That's my old shell,' Coral said.

I found my voice. 'So you just – climbed out of your shell?!'

'Yes. All crabs do,' Coral said. 'We moult our shells as we grow.'

I had a sudden thought. 'Is that why you've been so crabby?'

Coral nodded. 'I'm sorry. What with

everything else going on, I forgot I was going to moult soon. I feel SO much better now! Do you like my new shell?'

She twirled round. It was pink, spotty and very pretty. A **tidal wave** of relief hit me. I loved it. I loved her! I even loved Simon Trout!!!

'I do,' I said. 'And I'm really, REALLY glad I didn't kill you!'

'**HURRAH!**' A loud cheer erupted from the crowd, which faded as Simon Trout held up his clipboard.

There was a tense silence. Then. . .

'Simon says . . . Ten out of Ten!' he cried. The crowd went completely WILD!

Word of the Day: Yeeeee-haaaaaaaaa! This means 'I love everyone in the world!'

SPONGEDAY

I was woken up by a flock of angry seagulls
. . . no, it was just Coral singing at the top of
her voice. She was happier than I've ever
seen her, but I felt weirdly grumpy. Not even
watching Remy trying to lick a prawnflake off
his nose could cheer me up. Mum looked at me.

'What's wrong, Darcy?'

'I don't know,' I said. Because I didn't.

'Aren't you happy you won the Talent
Show?'

'Of course!' I was happy about that. But

something was bugging me . . .

'Well hurry up and eat your breakfast, sweetiefins. Coral's going home today, remember?'

When Mum said that, it hit me. I was actually going to miss Coral! It hadn't always been easy having her here – but I'd got used to her funny little ways. Even her crabbiness! Just then, she danced very uncrabbily into the kitchen.

'I can't WAIT to see Mum and Dad – and my brothers and sisters . . . Katy and Carmen and Kim and Colin and Kieran and Kevin and . . .'

'Goodness! How many brothers and sisters have you got?' Mum asked.

Coral started counting them off. . .

It took a long time . . .

. . .

. . .

. . .

'... and Crispin. Eight hundred and seventy-three.'

I blinked. 'Wow. I guess you'll never be lonely!'

'Sometimes it's a real pain,' Coral said.

'There are fifty of us to a bedroom. 'Sometimes I don't speak to Mum for days! And Dad gets us mixed up. He's forever calling me Chloe – so annoying!'

I laughed. 'Yeah, dads can be pretty a–'

'Amazing?' said Dad, coming in at that moment. 'I agree . . . anyway, Coral. Time to go.'

We swam to the school gates, where Walter Whale was waiting to take the pen pals home. There was lots of hugging and stuff. Angie was crying. Ozzie was all shades of blue.

I turned to Coral. 'I'll write every day.'

'You can come and stay,' Coral said. 'I'll ask Mum as soon as I get back.'

She climbed on to Walter with the others.

'Goodbye! We'll miss you!' everyone shouted.

As Walter swam away, I thought I could just see a pair of pink claws waving back at me out of the blue.

And then they were gone.

I felt a funny lump in my throat then.

Probably just a stuck prawnflake.

When I got home, I went into my bedroom to write a letter to Coral. But when I lay down on the bed I felt another funny lump. I looked under the covers.

It was Bertie – Coral's brain coral!

Attached to him was a note. It read:

DEAR DARCY,

I COULDN'T FIT BERTIE IN MY SUITCASE. I KNOW YOU'LL LOOK AFTER HIM WELL. AND NOW YOU'LL HAVE TO COME AND SEE ME SOON!

LOTS OF LOVE,

YOUR CRABBY FRIEND,

CORAL XXX

Word of the Day: SMILING

☺ ☺ ☺ ☺ ☺ ☺ ☺ ☺ ☺ ☺ ☺ ☺ ☺ ☺ ☺ ☺ ☺ ☺ ☺

Fishy facts!

Did you know...

Bottlenose dolphins are one of the
most intelligent animals on Earth, with
brains that are slightly bigger than
those of humans. They find food
and talk to each other using clicks
and whistles. Dolphins can make up to
1000 clicks per second!

Zombie crabs DO exist! A type of parasitic
barnacle survives by invading the bodies of
king crabs. Once inside the crab's brain the
barnacle can make the crab do
what it wants, even
making it behave like a
barnacle itself! Scary...

Octopuses have the biggest brains of all the invertebrates (animals with no backbone). They only keep a bit of their brain in their head though, the rest is in their arms. If an octopus loses an arm, the arm will still grab at food for up to an hour – but it can't eat it!

Turtles have been around a long time – about 200 million years in fact! They shared the planet with the very first dinosaurs. And they live a long time too, having about the same life span as humans.

Fishy Funnies!

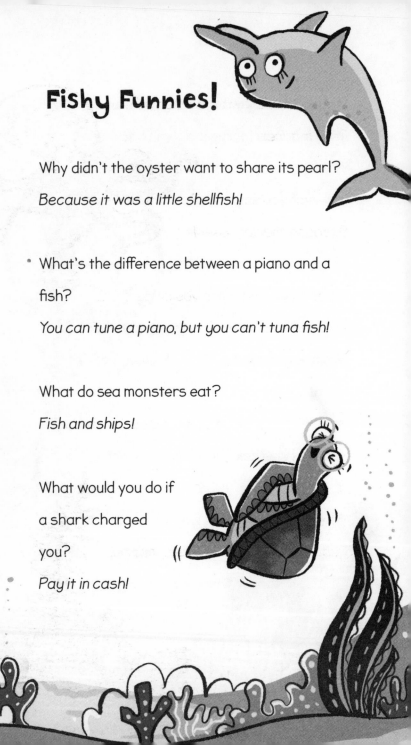

Why didn't the oyster want to share its pearl?

Because it was a little shellfish!

What's the difference between a piano and a fish?

You can tune a piano, but you can't tuna fish!

What do sea monsters eat?

Fish and ships!

What would you do if a shark charged you?

Pay it in cash!

What's the best way to catch a fish?

Drop it a line!

Why was the sand wet?

Because the sea weed!

What do you get when you cross a
school of fish with a herd of elephants?

Swimming trunks!

What sits at the bottom of the sea, twitching?

A nervous wreck!

Why is the ocean salty?

Pepper would make the fish sneeze!

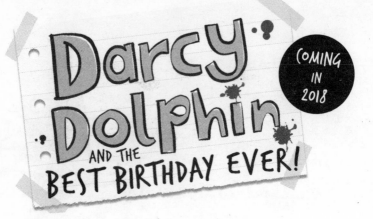

Darcy Dolphin AND THE **BEST BIRTHDAY EVER!**

COMING IN 2018

One last thing ...

don't forget to keep both of your

human eyes peeled for my

third **fintastic** diary.

I've joined the Sea Trouts, and

their motto is **Lend a Fin**.

Whether it's running pet exercise classes,

helping at the Retired Sharks Home

or planning your **best friend's**

birthday party, just ask me ...

the totally helpful Darcy Dolphin!